Football Crazy

Volume 1
Kick Off and Loss

by
Patrick John Naughton

Patrick Naughton

Dedicated to Kathy.

Published by Hamilton Naughton Publications

Copyright © P.J. Naughton 2023

P.J. Naughton has asserted his right under the Copyright, Designs and Patents Act 1988 to be identified as the author of this work.

This book is sold subject to the condition that it shall not, by way of trade or otherwise, be lent, resold, hired out, or otherwise circulated without the publisher's prior consent in any form of binding or cover other than that in which it is published and without a similar condition, including this condition, being imposed on the subsequent purchaser.

In this work of fiction, the characters, places and events are either the product of the author's imagination or they are used entirely fictitiously. Any resemblance to actual persons, living or dead, is purely coincidental.

All trade Marks are acknowledged.

Patrick Naughton

Football Crazy 1 - Kick Off And Loss

Introduction

Everybody knows how popular the game of football is amongst the general public. Over the years, vast amounts of money have been poured into the game which has added further to the interest. Football Crazy follows the exploits of a fictional club as it struggles to survive on the margins of the mad-cap world which football has become.

Goncaster United has enjoyed a very long history. Like many similar clubs, it came about when Queen Victoria was on the throne, when the railway reached the town, making it possible for local townsfolk to travel around the country to support their team. But despite all the years of endeavour, they've never really had much in the way of success to celebrate. Right up until the present day, the trophy cabinet has always remained empty. But despite their long history of upsets, the players and supporters remain resolute, clinging tenuously to a hope of success no matter how slim their chances might be.

Throughout their entire history, the club has faced some extremely stiff challenges. There has been war and economic recession, financial turmoil, pandemics and all types of disease not to mention countless injuries and suspensions amongst the many other trials and tribulations. But despite all the adversity, the club has continued to battle on and has somehow managed to persevere against the odds.

Along with all the other smaller clubs, their fight for survival continues to this present day. Every day these challenges only ever grow even bigger. Everyone involved in the club knows the score - they all have to dig deep if they are to have any possible hope of survival. Witness the thrills and spills and enjoy the true madness which is Football Crazy!

Patrick Naughton

Contents

Introduction 1
1. The Kick Off 5
2. Cooking Up A Storm 8
3. The Warm Up 11
4. Parousia 13
5. Reaching For Glory 17
6. A Terrible Foul 19
7. The Tumult 20
8. Staff Meeting 21
9. Helping Out At The Menagerie 23
10. The Arrest 24
11. Final Preparations 25
12. A Final Journey 26
13. Unlucky For Some 28
14. A Service To Remember 31
15. The Day Of Reckoning. 34
16. A Fitting Memorial 37

Patrick Naughton

Football Crazy 1 - Kick Off And Loss

1. The Kick Off

THE USUAL MOANS spread throughout the sparse home crowd as the latest game moved towards yet another depressing conclusion. Expressions of another agonizing loss were etched across the faces of all the locals. It had been yet another dismal display - a series of missed passes, a few feeble shots that were all way off target, and a catalogue of defensive blunders that together provided precious little cause for any cheer from the dark, dismal home stands on this cold, damp miserable Saturday afternoon. Groaning was about the only defence the home supporters had against the biting cold.

Kenneth, the largest goalkeeper in the league, panicked as a long looping shot was fired high up into the air towards him. 'I've got this, it's mine, keep back!' he screamed, as he manhandled the defenders in front of him and pushed them out of the way. The ball bounced high a few yards in front of him. He lunged desperately towards it but missed and yet again it bounced inexorable into the back of the net. The crowd groaned in disgust.

Kenneth flailed his arms around alike a madman and shouted at the defenders, 'What kind of defending do you call that?'

But despite all his histrionics, it was just another vain attempt to hide his obvious embarrassment. Nobody doubted where the fault lay.

Over in the Goncaster dugout, beads of sweat formed across the forehead of Les the Manager. 'Not again,' he groaned to Doug the trainer who shook his head in despair.

'Another six nil,' replied Doug, 'I can't believe it. We're being slaughtered again.'

'We'll be going down if we carry on like this, mark my words. This'll not go down well with Mr Shufflebottom, I can guarantee that.'

Les's mobile phone suddenly lit up. He glanced at the screen in dread, fully aware how quick bad news travels. He didn't want to answer it, but he knew he had no choice, he was the boss and as such it was his job to face the consequences. He took a deep breath and summoning all his strength, he managed to bring a weak smile to his lips before answering, 'Hello Mr Shufflebottom. Yes Mr Shufflebottom. Of course, Mr Shufflebottom. I think so Mr Shufflebottom. Yes Mr Shufflebottom. Very good Mr Shufflebottom. I will do Mr Shufflebottom. Of course, Mr Shufflebottom. Thank you, Mr Shufflebottom.'

Les's face dropped as he put the phone down.

'Who was that?' asked Doug, hoping beyond hope that it wasn't what he feared.

'Well, it wasn't the Prime Minister phoning to offer us a knighthood I can tell you that for nothing.'

Doug shuddered. He felt even more embarrassed now.

'It was Mr Shufflebottom, our illustrious owner. He's coming to see our next match.'

'What do you think he wants?' asked Doug, fearing the very worst.

'Well, I doubt he'll be driving all the way up from Colchester to give us all a pay rise. What do you think?'

Doug gulped hard trying to control his fear, 'I expect not. Not after the fifth straight loss in a row.'

'I hope I'm wrong, but if I were you, I'd prepare for the worst. Mr Shufflebottom hasn't been up here for years. The last time he was here he sacked all the entire management team.'

Out on the pitch the inadequacies of the home team were plainly on display for all to see. Yet another shot was fired at the Goncaster goal. This time the ball flew like a cannon ball straight for the middle of the goal. Kenneth failed to react quick enough. He stepped back over the goal line in a forlorn attempt to avoid the shot, but it hit him full square in the groin with a sickening thud. Seven nil! He could hear the jeers as he doubled up in pain, trying desperately to breathe through the agony as he clutched his private parts, hoping he might at the very least engender some sympathy. But alas he only endured further disappointment.

As the rest of the fans fell silent, it was left to the oldest fan in the home stands to deliver the unanimous verdict, 'Absolute bloody rubbish. You're not a patch on your grandfather. He knew his way round a football pitch. Not like you shower.'

These comments occasioned a wry cheer from the crowd, a rare moment of levity on an otherwise dismal afternoon. Mr Drinkall, or Stan as he was affectionately known by everyone at the club, was nearly ninety years old. He'd been a supporter at the club since he was a young boy and despite suffering from a bewildering list of health issues, he'd attended every game since time immemorial.

Kenneth couldn't take any more. He'd had enough for one day. As he was helped off the pitch limping, a young substitute was put in goal in his place.

'Not another injury,' groaned Les.

'I'd better go check him out,' said Doug.

Doug followed Kenneth as he hobbled awkwardly into the changing room helped by two young ballboys. He was clearly in a lot of pain. 'You need to sit down,' said Doug.

'I'll be alright,' replied Kenneth wincing, 'Just give me a minute.' But no one was convinced that he was going to be alright. Afterall, no one could remember ever seeing Kenneth looking *alright*. But now he looked worse than ever. He was pale and drawn and he looked distinctly unwell.

'You've been badly winded,' said Doug.

'I couldn't stay on. It's not just this.'

'I was concerned when I saw how it hit you. How are you getting on with things, you know, with that little problem that we talked about? I guess this won't have helped any?'

'I'm afraid them pills you gave me didn't help at all.'

'I can only apologize Kenneth. They usually do the trick. I know quite a few people who swear by them. I'm really sorry.'

'Not to worry,' replied Kenneth, 'There's no hard feelings on my side.'

'Try not to let it get you down. You've just got to keep your pecker up.'

'Chance would be a fine thing.'

'Did you say you had another problem?

'Oh Doc, I'm absolutely exhausted. I can't tell you. I've got the runs. Not just a bit. It's terrible. Really, really bad.'

'You haven't been eating in the canteen again, have you?' asked Doug.

'Of course I have. Where else can we eat? We haven't all got wives at home who cook you know! And you know how Les doesn't like us nipping down the pub every day.'

'Well, you know how careful you've got to be with the food in there.'

'It started on Wednesday. I had some of Brenda's prune and liquorice tart. It was only a very small portion.'

'And how are things now?'

'It's terrible. I haven't been able to stop going to the toilet since. I don't think I'll be able to play the next match. Not the full ninety minutes anyway. Not unless things improve. I'd never have lasted out there today if this hadn't happened. No way.'

'You can't let us down,' said Doug, 'You know how important these cup games are. The BBC Match-of-the-Day cameras will be here and everything. And the owner's coming up. I'm not messing. It's imperative, all our careers are on the line. We've really got to field our very best team. There's no doubt about that.'

'How am I ever going to get through it?'

'Trust me, just don't think about it and you'll be fine. Try to drink plenty of bottled water. But don't drink anything out of the tap. Certainly not in this place. With luck you'll soon get over it.'

'I'm really badly bruised,' said Kenneth as he gasped in pain.

'I'll stoke the boiler. There'll be hot water in about twenty minutes. You can have a bath. That'll make you feel better.'

'Hot water?' shrieked Kenneth, 'Are you kidding? That'd be a first. We're lucky if it's even tepid. I can't remember ever getting into hot water in this place.'

'Well let's hope it stays that way,' said Doug as he picked up a coal skuttle and tipped it into the boiler. Clouds of smoke came billowing out and filled the entire changing room. Kenneth disappeared for a few seconds then emerged coughing, 'That chimney hasn't been cleaned for years.'

'We can't get a chimney sweep anymore. I'll have to get hold of some brushes and see what Shameless can make of it.'

'God help us. I think I'd rather put up with cold water.'

2. Cooking Up A Storm

AS ALWAYS, on the morning of the match Brenda and Daisy were stupidly busy in the canteen. Brenda was up to her armpits preparing food, whilst Daisy helped her out in between serving the few customers who ventured into the establishment at such an early hour.

'It never ceases to amaze me who comes into this place so early in a morning,' said Daisy, 'And the things they ask for!'

'If you listen to Les, the way things are at the moment we need every single penny we can get.'

'Are things that bad?'

'Never been worse he reckons.'

A young man approached the counter. 'What would you like love?' asked Daisy.

'Can I have a Margarita pizza please?'

'Certainly. Do you want any extras?' Daisy always blushed when she asked that question, it seemed so open to misinterpretation but she knew she simply had to ask.

'No,' replied the youth, 'But can I have it without cheese.'

'Of course.'

'And no tomatoes.'

Daisy handed over a pizza base on a plate with no topping on it. She took his money looking somewhat further embarrassed.

Brenda noticed Daisy's blushes, 'Les has asked us to pull out all the stops. We need to impress today of all days. He's hoping to win Mr Shufflebottom over to make some sort of big investment.'

Brenda carefully unpacked a box of biscuits marked 'Reject' and put them one by one into a box marked 'Finest West Country biscuits'.

'I'm doing my signature dish,' boasted Brenda, 'I'm sure my meat and potato pie will win him over, if anything can.'

Football Crazy 1 - Kick Off And Loss

Brenda lifted a massive pie dish out of the fridge. It had pastry neatly arranged across the bottom and up the sides. She placed the vessel onto a work surface and proceeded to scoop meat and potatoes into it from a large bubbling cauldron.

'That looks lovely,' said Daisy.

'We need to impress in the canteen because, god knows, no one will ever be impressed anywhere else.'

Daisy lifted a huge cauldron off the stove and peered into it. She stirred the contents with a long wooden spoon, 'There's a lot of this liquorice pie left over. It's such a shame to bin it when there's so many homeless people going short of food these days.'

'Nay we can't waste it with the way things are. We haven't got money to chuck away you know. There's nowt wrong with it. Stir it into the mash, it'll bulk it out and add a bit of flavour.'

Daisy scooped the liquorice mix into a large taurine containing mash and mixed it in with the wooden spoon. 'It's giving it a lovely colour.'

Brenda unwrapped a couple of slaps of butter and threw them into the pan and poured in a pint of milk as Daisy continued to work the mixture. After a few minutes Daisy licked her fingers as she admired the results of her labour. 'It's certainly got an exotic flavour. I'm sure that'll be a winner whatever happens on the pitch.'

Another customer, this time a middle-aged chap appeared at the counter.

'Can I have a full English breakfast please love, without eggs, no mushrooms and no beans please?'

'What about sausage and hash browns?'

'No thank you very much.'

Daisy gave the punter a plate with two slices of bacon on it and a piece of toast. 'That's eight ninety-nine please sir.'

The customer handed over a ten-pound note and walked away without saying anything further. He hadn't bothered to collect his change and despite all her efforts, Daisy couldn't help but notice his derision.

'What's Mr Shufflebottom like?' Daisy asked Brenda nervously, slightly concerned that she might have just met him unexpectedly.

'Well, I haven't seen him for ages. He's tall and slim, elderly, very elderly really, white hair, well-to-do, very well spoken.'

'He could be at a funny age,' said Daisy.

'To be honest, I think he's always been at a funny age,' said Brenda.

'In my experience, most men are.'

'He's a real gent really to be fair. Done very well for himself. Loaded, owns some factories down in Kent somewhere; steel mills, foundries, that kind of thing.'

'His wife must be very lucky,' said Daisy admiringly as thoughts of endless shopping trips flashed briefly across her mind.

'Oh, he's never married. He hasn't got any family of any kind. That sort never do. Always been too busy I suppose.'

'Do you think he might be gay?'

'He's definitely a ladies' man. Had more women than hot dinners.'

'I think Kenneth was hoping he might bat for both sides,' said Daisy.

'Just wishful thinking on his part. But play your cards right and you never know. I'm certain he'd make somebody a perfect husband.'

'I doubt I could ever impress him with my lack of football knowledge,' sighed Daisy.

'I don't think he's that interested in football to be honest.

'We might have a chance then,' Daisy smiled cheekily. 'Why does he own a club then if he's not that bothered about football?'

'I suppose people like him just use football for publicity. Everybody knows his name. Without football he'd be a total unknown.'

Two more customers came up to the counter. This time scruffily dressed unshaven student types.

'Do you have a fat rascal?' asked the taller student.

'We've got Kenneth in goal,' grinned Daisy.

'We've got more than one if truth be known,' added Brenda, 'But not one that you'd want I'm afraid.'

'We've got tea-cakes and a nice range of pastries,' said Daisy.

The customer sighed, 'I'll just have a Latte... without milk please.'

Daisy paused for a second then started to prepare a black coffee when the second student spoke up, 'Excuse me. Is Garlic bread cheaper if it's ordered without Garlic?'

Bang! Daisy was just wondering how to reply when there was an almighty crash. The kitchen window suddenly exploded as a football flew through it. Everybody ducked for cover as shards of broken glass few in all directions.

'Christ almighty!' said the first student as he grimaced in shock.

'Good Heavens,' said Daisy.

'That'll be Joey,' said Brenda as she picked pieces of glass out of the pie she was making, 'He's a fabulous striker but a total bloody nuisance. I can always tell when it's him breaking a window. He's got such a wonderful left foot.'

'We can't serve that now,' said Daisy frowning at the surface of the pie that Brenda was picking glass from.

'Nonsense,' said Brenda, 'It'll be alright. It's just a few bits of glass. Nobody will notice. It's never done anybody any harm before. Besides, we haven't got enough ingredients to make another one and we haven't got time, Mr Shufflebottom will be here soon.'

Kenneth rushed into the canteen breathless and red-faced, 'Can we have our ball back?'

'Young Joey can't half belt it,' said Brenda.

'Joey? It wasn't Joey,' said Kenneth, 'It was young Neville.'

'Neville? That little sod! Well, you can tell him if he does that again I'll be coming out there to sort him out.'

Kenneth glanced up at the clock on the canteen wall, 'Is it really that time already?'

Daisy nodded, 'Nearly midday.'

'I might as well have my lunch - beat the rush.'

'We've got some pasta and chicken,' said Daisy, 'Doug is keen you all bulk up on carbs. He reckons it'll give you all more energy out on the field.'

'I can't be doing with anything like that,' said Kenneth, 'I fancy egg and chips but no, I'll be good for once. I'll have sausage and mash. I must be at the top of my game today of all days.'

'We've got some lovely mash. I've just made it. Take a seat, I'll bring it over.'

Daisy dished out a generous portion of sausage and mash and took it over to Kenneth who had taken up a seat at the end of a long Formica topped wooden table.

'That looks fabulous,' said Kenneth.

'It contains our secret ingredient,' said Daisy, 'It'll give you all a bit of extra umph.'

Kenneth took a mouthful, 'Whatever it is, it tastes gorgeous. We need all the help we can get against these Blues. You know what they're like.'

'They were a rowdy bunch last time they came,' said Daisy.

'They're certainly a physical side. They left me black and blue last time they came. If we win, I'll dedicate the victory to this wicked dinner and you lovely ladies.'

Daisy smiled as she wheeled away back to the counter carrying an empty tray. Kenneth scoffed down his massive lunch with his usual enthusiasm. He always put more energy into eating than he ever put into anything out on the field.

3. The Warm Up

OUT ON THE PITCH the rest of the team were warming up in preparation for the big game. The crowd was beginning to gather. Despite their sparse numbers, there was a certain growing frisson amongst the regulars. They were all fully aware that television cameras were being setup. This was a rare occurrence for such a lowly team and as such it generated a good deal of excitement as it ensured they'd see clips of their team on the T.V. And given the modest attendance expected, it was highly likely the fans would all see themselves on the box as well. Some of the fans had seen themselves on T.V. many times before, but the prospect of another glimpse of themselves never failed to provide a thrill.

Doug, the trainer was also aware of the cameras. This was a rare chance to showcase his talent. He rolled a ball back out onto the pitch to his players and issued an instruction more to the cameras than to his players, 'Keep it tight at the back and don't forget, play your diamonds.'

The young players ignored him but he tried to exude confidence as he strode over to take a seat between Shameless and Les who were intently watching proceedings from the dugout.

'Brenda isn't very keen on Neville is she?' asked Doug.

'Hardly surprising really,' said Les, 'Neville's Dad was the copper who arrested Brenda's son Terry.'

'That were five years ago,' said Shameless.

'They must have long memories round here,' said Doug.

'Long memories?' said Les, 'Well he is still inside you know.'

'What did he do?' asked Doug.

'He did everything,' said Shameless.

'It'd be easier to tell you what he didn't do,' said Les. 'Affray for a start.'

'I'm surprised it was only one,' said Shameless.

'Theft,' said Les, 'Assault. ABH. GBH. Robbery with and without menaces.'

'Menaces with menaces,' said Shameless.

'He was a monster,' said Les, 'An absolute animal. He's the reason your predecessor left.'

'He still on our books you know,' said Doug.

'He is,' said Les, 'But I don't think they'll let him out anytime soon.'

'He got ten years,' said Shameless.

'Well, with good behaviour...,' said Doug.

'Good behaviour? From Terry Tight Eyes? There's no chance,' said Les.

Shameless laughed, 'He'll be doing drugs and all sorts.'

'Was he any good?' asked Doug.

'Memorable,' said Les, 'Very good at marking players.'

'He marked most of them for life,' said Shameless. 'There's people still walking around with the injuries they got when they tried to play against him.'

'And some of them still aren't walking,' said Les. 'He had loads of starts for us. Longest he stayed on the pitch was about ten minutes. He got red carded every time.'

'He was alright until somebody tried to tackle him,' said Shameless.

'Or looked at him,' said Les. 'Then he was in there, fists flying, head butts, biting, gouging, the lot. He was like a mad dog on acid.'

'Last game he played here, he bit the ref's ear off,' said Shameless.

'I wouldn't mind so much but he'd bitten his other ear off earlier in the season,' said Les.

'What happened?' asked Doug, 'I bet he was in big trouble?

'Well, he would have been,' said Les, 'But the disciplinary *hearing* kept getting postponed.'

'For technical reasons,' said Shameless, 'The ref couldn't lip read.'

'Then he got picked up by the law. I wouldn't have him back anyway,' said Les, 'Even if they did let him out. No way. And I doubt Mr Shufflebottom would have him back either. Talking of which he'll be here soon.'

Les glanced across the field at the players who were passing the ball around very half-heartedly. He sighed heavily when he caught sight of Joey leaning up against a goalpost smoking, 'This lot could do with a bit of aggression.'

Doug was embarrassed. 'Come on you lot. Show some commitment,' he shouted, 'Where's your aggression?'

4. Parousia

A BRAND-NEW BENTLEY rolled majestically through the main gates. The hue of British racing green shone across the car park. A smart looking chauffeur in a tailored black suit and a matching peak cap opened the rear door of the vehicle and Mr Shufflebottom stepped serenely on to the tarmac. He glanced up at the façade of the stadium before walking through the main entrance where he was met by Les.

'Thank you for coming up to see us Mr Shufflebottom sir,' said Les, 'It's lovely to see you. I don't know if you've met Mr Drinkall before?'

'I don't believe I've had the pleasure.'

'Stan is our oldest fan.'

'Pleased to meet you sir,' said Stan.

'I was one of the players back in the day, I played right-back under your grandfather.'

'You look like you still know a thing or two,' said Mr Shufflebottom, 'And what year was it that you finally hung up your boots?'

'I broke my leg in December 1967. I was forty. Players didn't retire so young in those days.'

'And I bet you carried on working?'

'They finished me from the brickyard about twenty years ago, after I had my first heart-attack.'

'I've had a heart-attack as well,' said Mr Shufflebottom, 'In fact I've had three.'

'I've had five heart-attacks,' said Stan.

'Gosh you have been busy..'

'I've had two strokes as well,' boasted Stan, 'I'm on twenty-six tablets now. I was on thirty-two but I've got my blood pressure down now.'

'Well done! I'm on twenty-one,' said Mr Shufflebottom, 'Well thank you for being such a gallant supporter and do enjoy the game.'

As Stan wandered off, Les introduced Mr Shufflebottom to Doug before they all went through to the canteen.

'We'd like to take the opportunity to walk you through our plans, if possible, sir,' said Les.

'To improve results out on the field,' added Doug. Mr Shufflebottom nodded.

'Maybe after the match,' said Les, 'It's all coming together at long last. We just need to make a few minor tweaks to the team.'

'Decisions!' said Mr Shufflebottom, 'It's all about decisions. It's the same for you guys in sport as it is for those of us in business. You always need to have consistency every time; good quality decisions and you need to reach them as quickly as possible.'

'I think you'll not find us wanting in that regard Mr Shufflebottom,' said Les trying his best to exude an air of confidence.

'The thing is gents,' said Mr Shufflebottom, 'There are some big changes in the offing. And I wanted to see you face to face to explain everything to you.'

The three men sat down at a table which had been specially reserved for them. It was draped with a red and white checked linen tablecloth; the sort you'd expect to find in a superior Parisian bistro. Both Brenda and Daisy came over to attend to their special VIP guest. Daisy curtsied whilst Brenda wheeled over the large pie on a serving trolley. Daisy held plates out whilst Brenda served out the pie along with garden peas and generous portions of their special mash.

Les slid a bottle of sparking rose wine out of an ice bucket expertly positioned at the centre of the table and poured wine into crystal glasses first for Mr Shufflebottom, then for Doug and finally for himself.

'Good health!' said Les as he raised his glass.

'Bottoms up!' said Doug.

Mr Shufflebottom took a sip from his glass, 'I shouldn't really, not with all the tablets, but I have to say, a very nice choice Les.'

'Do you know what dessert you'll be wanting gents?' asked Daisy, 'It's Lemon drizzle or chocolate fudge cake?'

'Lemon drizzle for me please young lady,' said Mr Shufflebottom, 'It sounds delicious.'

'And for you gents?'

Les was flummoxed, 'Er, I'll have... well, I'd say...er.'

Daisy began to panic at her boss's inability to reach a decision. She tried her best to divert attention, 'Doug? Which would you like?'

'Oooh, it's a tricky one that love.'

'I'll come back later,' she said and with that she sidled away back to the counter, concerned that she might have inadvertently exposed a weakness in the organisation.

Mr Shufflebottom glanced sidewards. He'd clearly noted the lack of decisiveness amongst his management. *If they can't decide what dessert they want, how can they make the tough decisions necessary to run a football team?*

The three men tucked into their lunch.

'Are you intending to stay with us for long Stephen?' asked Les.

'The thing is Les, things haven't been going quite so well of late. Financially we've reached the end of the road.'

'Surely! A man like you must have a few bob in the bank with all that steel your company makes and everything,' said Les.

Mr Shufflebottom shook his head. 'We're lucky to clear five hundred pounds a ton these days. That's when we can sell it.'

'Five hundred pounds! That doesn't sound too bad. I imagine you make hundreds of tons of the stuff,' said Doug.

'These days that doesn't even cover the cost of energy,' said Mr Shufflebottom, 'Let alone the wage bill or the raw materials.'

'You must have millions of pounds worth of assets though,' said Les, 'A man of your distinction.'

'I'd probably be worth millions if I didn't have any debt,' said Mr Shufflebottom, 'But these days the debt is at least ten times bigger than the value of the assets.'

'That sounds a bit grim,' said Doug.

'What about next door?' asked Les, 'You must do alright there?'

'The zoo? I lose almost as much next door as I lose in this club.'

'Surely, it can't cost that much,' said Les, 'The lovely Laura practically runs it single handed. Her wages can't be that high?'

'It's not the wage bill Les, it's the cost of keeping all the animals. The food bill is enormous and then there's the vet bills. Only last week it cost me five grand to get dentures for the alligator.'

'That doesn't sound good,' said Les.

'The truth is gentlemen; the free lunches are coming to an end. I thought it best if you heard it direct from me. I've really got no choice; I've had to put the club up for sale.'

'As bad as that?' said Les.

'Do you think anyone will be interested, in buying us like?' asked Doug.

Mr Shufflebottom poked the food on the plate in front of him with a fork, 'Well to be honest, it's never going to be a purely commercial transaction. Any organisation that loses ten grand a month is only ever going to have limited appeal amongst the business community.'

Les was taken aback by this announcement. Mr Shufflebottom frowned more deeply, 'Is there glass in this food?

'No not at all,' said Doug, 'It's sea salt. Brenda always uses the finest ingredients.'

'The best chefs always season food appropriately,' said Les.

The three men continued to eat in silence. Both Les and Doug were surprised by what they'd just heard and wondered if there was anything they could say to turn the situation around in any way.

Mr Shufflebottom wondered how the news would go down with the players and the rest of the staff. He didn't want anybody to leave that might impact the future viability of the club, but he felt he'd had no choice but to break the news on the precarious financial position of the club. He was just wondering if he should provide more details about the chaotic state of his financial affairs when he suddenly found himself short of breath. He grimaced. Sweat trickled down his face and he clutched his stomach as agonizing pains shot down from his chest into the lower reaches of his abdomen.

'Do excuse me gents. I seem to have the most terrible stomach cramps.'

'It's only to be expected Mr Shufflebottom,' said Doug, 'It'll be the excitement at the prospect of seeing the performance of the scintillating team that we're putting out today.'

Les flashed Doug an unbelieving glance. Knowing the level of fitness of the players and the extent of their abilities, he didn't want expectations to be set too high.

Mr Shufflebottom nodded towards the loo. 'I'll be back shortly.' And with that he staggered off towards the restroom.

Once their VIP was out of earshot, Les turned to Doug and said, 'Don't eat any more of this pie for Christ's sake! It's absolutely full of broken glass.'

'I wondered what it was,' said Doug, 'Let's get out there and make sure they're getting on OK with the warm up.'

5. Reaching For Glory

OUT ON THE FIELD, Kenneth was struggling to get a ball down from the guttering that ran along the roof of the stand behind the goal.

'We've got enough balls,' shouted Doug, 'You can leave that one up there.'

'There's no way that I'm having that thing hanging up there behind me. I've got enough distractions as it is.'

Doug grabbed a long flagpole off one of the young cheerleaders and used it to poke the ball out of the gutter. The ragged looking ball fell back behind the goal. A small ballboy kicked it back onto the pitch as the team carried on with their warmup routine; jogging around, stretching and passing a number of balls to each other in a seemingly random display.

'We really ought to get another set of balls,' said Doug.

'We'd be better off with another team,' said Les, 'But the way things are looking, I wouldn't hold out much hope. I don't know what the gaffer will make of this lot... if he ever comes out of the bog that is.'

Doug looked at his watch. Realising that kick-off time was fast approaching, he said to Shameless, 'Hey Shameless! Go and see how His Royal Highness is getting on in the gents. Tell him it's nearly time for kick-off.'

Shameless duly went off to find Mr Shufflebottom.

On the field the team continued their warm up. Several of the players were clearly up for the challenge. The ball was flicked to Joey in front of goal. He steadied it. Kenneth shook visibly in his goal as he focussed on the shot which was about to come his way. Joey smashed the ball with his right foot. Kenneth lunged at it but missed. The net behind Kenneth bulged as the ball flew into the goal.

'Offside!' shouted Kenneth, 'That was way off that was. You're not getting away with that.'

Kenneth ran up to Joey and tried to push him.

'What are you doing you plonker?' protested Joey as he sidestepped Kenneth's attack.

Les was dismayed. He jumped out of his seat, 'Hey! You two clowns! When you've finished! Remember we're trying to impress!'

Kenneth turned away to retrieve the ball out of the goal, muttering all the time under his breath.

As Les sat back in his seat, Shameless returned. Les could see that Shameless was in a state of serious distress. Not much ever bothered Shameless, so Les knew something was clearly very wrong.

'Is everything alright?' asked Les.

'He's gone!' said Shameless.

'Gone?' asked Doug, 'What do you mean he's gone?

'He's passed,' said Shameless.

'Passed?' asked Doug, 'How can he have passed? He hasn't even been playing.'

Shameless felt the weight of dread descend on to him, 'He's croaked. He's ceased to exist. He's kicked the bucket. He's pegged it. Bit the dust. Popped his clogs. Deceased. Expired. Passed away. He's been taken. He's shuffled off his mortal coil. He's gone to a better place. Perished. Met his end. He's breathed his last'.

'You mean he's dead?' asked Les.

'As dead as a dodo,' said Shameless, 'Elvis has left the building.'

'Bloody hell. What are we going to do now?' asked Doug.

'Have you called an ambulance?' asked Les.

'St John's have looked at him,' said Shameless. 'There's nowt they can do. Nobody can.'

'Well, that's put the mockers on it, that has,' said Les.

Kenneth heard the fuss and walked over with a ball in his hands, 'Is everything alright?'

'We've only gone and killed off our one and only benefactor,' said Les.

'Who? Mr Shufflebottom? Dead?' asked Kenneth.

'Keep it quiet,' said Les, 'Until we work out what to do.'

'Has he been helping us out?' asked Kenneth.

'He's only been stumping up ten grand each and every month to pay our bills for more years than I care to remember, that's all,' said Les.

'Maybe his family will help out instead?' said Doug.

'Family?' said Les, 'What family? He hasn't got a family. You don't think a man would pump money into a place like this if he had any family, do you? He was a confirmed bachelor. We're his family. And he was our only hope. We've had it now.'

'Should we cancel the match?' asked Doug.

'What and lose the takings?' said Les, 'You've got to be joking.'

Doug knew it was important to galvanize the team. 'Come on Kenneth, time to take your place between the sticks. Let's do this one in memory of Mr Shufflebottom.'

Kenneth came over all faint. 'I need the loo.'

'It's just shock,' said Les.

'You haven't got time for anything like that now,' said Doug, 'You've already been. It's all in your mind. *Just don't think about it.* Come on now big fella. Focus! Keep your mind on the game.'

The teams lined up for the obligatory photo before the ref tossed the coin. Then Doug signalled to the team to take their places ready for the kick-off. Both teams spread out into position and glancing at his watch the ref promptly blew his whistle to signal the kick-off.

'I can't stand to watch this,' said Les, 'I'll be in my office.' And with that Les strutted off to his office. Within seconds the opposition striker collected the ball on the halfway line, ran down the field and scored. The away crowd threw dozens of toilet-rolls on to the pitch. On seeing all this toilet tissue, Kenneth was suddenly struck by panic. Instinct took over. He had no choice. He ran towards the tunnel like a madman. He desperately clutched his backside but to no avail, unfortunately he didn't get very far...

6. A Terrible Foul

DOUG BURST INTO LES'S OFFICE to report what had just occurred out on the pitch. Les had barely had time to get comfortable behind his desk. 'What is it this time?'
'It's Kenneth he's got a red card.'
'Sent off? So soon? What was he doing for God's sake?'
'He's fouled,' said Doug, struggling to find the best words to describe what he'd just seen.
'Who did he foul?' asked Les.
Doug was embarrassed, 'The pitch!'
'The pitch? What are you talking about? How on Earth can he foul a pitch? Oh no! You don't mean?'
'I'm afraid so. To be fair he's had the runs all week. I thought he'd got over the worst of it. I wouldn't have put him out there otherwise.'

Les and Doug look at the replay of the sending off on the large TV monitor in the corner of Les's office. They watch as the opposition score their goal. Then Kenneth is seen running towards the touchline holding his bottom. Before he gets to the sideline he stops running, pulls down his shorts and does a poo in front of the entire crowd. The two men watch the screen in despair as they see the referee run up to Kenneth brandishing the red card. A linesman joins in. He's seen shouting angrily at Kenneth and pointing down the tunnel, ordering him to leave the pitch. The red-faced Kenneth is extremely flustered and tries to argue back.

The commentary is excruciating. 'These are extraordinary scenes. We've never seen anything like this before. After losing their last six games *on the trot*, it seems Goncaster United have *gone down the pan again*.'

Kenneth looked suitably embarrassed and very flustered. The two men watch in horror as they see him pick up one of the loo rolls from the pitch to wipe his bottom. As he does so the camera closes in on him.

'This is a team that really need to do something about their *movement* off the ball,' continued the commentator.

Eventually Kenneth desperately pulls up his shorts before strutting off in total embarrassment down the tunnel. 'Bloody hell,' said Les, 'This'll go viral. We'll never live this down. How the hell are we going to find an investor now?'

'I don't know if we'll ever get over this,' said Doug.

'The way things are going, we'll be lucky to last to the end of the month,' sighed Les, 'If they hold any kind of inquest on Mr S, it could be curtains for the lot of us.'

7. The Tumult

IT WAS UNUSUAL for Laura to be seen in the canteen in the middle of the day. Nobody had ever seen her in such a state before. Everyone knew her as the most serene paragon of beauty. They'd never seen her in total distress. Things took a turn for the worse when she caught sight of Brenda and Daisy who were also crying.

'Mum! What going on?'

'Oh Laura, I can't believe what's happened,' said Brenda, 'It's terrible.'

'Why? What have you done?'

'We've killed Mr Shufflebottom,' said Daisy.

'And I'll miss Tallulah's wedding now,' said Brenda.

'Well, it isn't like it's her first-time round, is it?' said Daisy, snivelling and trying but failing to hold back the tears, 'I mean, it's not like you haven't seen her walk down the aisle before.'

'This is number six, isn't it?' said Laura.

'Five for silver, six for gold,' said Daisy. 'Who'd have thought? A golden wedding at such a tender age.'

'Well let's hope she does a bit better with golden boy than she did with hiho silver,' said Brenda.

'Did that last marriage not work out so well then?' asked Daisy.

'It seemed to start off OK,' said Laura, 'Until matey boy disappeared very sudden like.'

'With a load of fancy stuff, he'd picked up from the jewellers. Probably silver I shouldn't wonder,' said Brenda.

'No body has seen him since,' said Laura. 'Especially not Tallulah. But plenty of people are on the lookout for him.'

'The police mainly,' said Brenda.

'The Met have been asking about him,' said Laura.

Suddenly Tallulah bustled in through the canteen door like a gunslinging cowboy walking into a saloon. She was carrying a bulging "Next" carrier bag. The top of her bulging left shoulder was covered with a polythene patch which barely covered a glowing raw wound where a brand-new tattoo had been inscribed earlier that morning. Laura rolled her eyes which she always did whenever she encountered her heavily tattooed and badly pierced half-sister.

It wouldn't have been nearly so bad if it had been done tastefully, she wasn't totally against body art per se, in fact she had some discrete artwork of her own. What she particularly didn't like about Tallulah's tats was that she always had it done at a cut-price place behind the market, by a man who used poor quality inks which produced the most horrible illuminous colours. He used these to create the most hideous designs - geometric shapes that were wonky, words that weren't evenly spaced made up of letters of different sizes, that sort of thing. They were just scribbles, rather than any kind of artwork.

Tallulah projected a fearsome streetwise persona, something that was in sharp contrast to Laura's glowing porcelain beauty.

'There's no way am I going ahead, not without you being there Mam,' screamed Tallulah, 'He were past it anyway. How can they blame you for him being such a wimp?'

'I am sorry love, truly I am,' said Brenda, 'Causing all this worry at a time like this.' Then pointing at Tallulah's shopping bag, she said, 'Is that your head-dress?'

'It is and it'll keep,' said Tallulah, 'I'm going to postpone everything until you get out.'

'Ooh I don't know. Do you think that's really wise?' asked Daisy.

'Do you really think Daz will wait that long?' asked Brenda.

Tallulah shrugged, 'Well if he doesn't it's his loss.'

Brenda could see that despite all Tallulah's attempts to look hard, she too was clearly very upset by everything that had happened. Brenda put her arm around Tallulah and cuddled her.

Laura broke the silence, 'I've had a word with Les. He's sending Shameless round to help take care of the animals until all this is over. So, we'll both be able to take care of you Mum.'

'Oh, I am lucky to have you,' sniffed Brenda, 'I don't know what I'd do without you both.'

8. Staff Meeting

AFTER THE MATCH Les called all the staff together for a meeting. He wasn't entirely certain how things would play out but he felt it was best to make sure they were all up to speed with recent events.

'Thank you all for coming together at such short notice,' said Les, 'I thought it best that we got together at this very difficult time.'

'Was it the pie?' asked Kenneth.

On hearing this question Daisy began to sob.

'Try not to dwell on any of that love,' said Les, 'I expect there'll be an inquest. The police will want to take statements, I'm certain we'll get a chance to put our side of the story.'

'Can't we just lie?' asked Shameless, 'Tell them he'd had lunch before he got here?'

'That'll only make matters worse,' said Doug. 'They'll have forensics and all sorts. We just need to stick to the truth.'

'But don't answer any questions they don't ask,' said Les. 'The less we say, the better.'

'What are we going to do about the arrangements?' asked Kenneth. 'He didn't have any family you know.'

'I've asked Doug here to make all the arrangements,' said Les, 'Once the coroner has released the body, we'll make sure he gets the sendoff he deserves.'

'It's a pity your Terry isn't here,' Kenneth shouted across to Brenda, 'Afterall, nobody knows more about send-offs than him.'

Les told Kenneth to behave and then asked if there were any questions. He scanned the room but all he saw were blank faces except for Doug who was busily texting on his phone.

'Doug! What's so important that you have to text at a time like this? Have some respect man.'

'I'm just texting the undertakers. They've asked for an inscription for the grave.'

'Bloody hell, the body isn't cold yet. Can't you write a letter for once in your life?'

'Mr Shufflebottom won't mind,' countered Doug, 'We've got a lot to do if we're going to arrange the funeral in time.'

'Before we all get sent down?' asked Shameless.

'I'm all in favour of getting this over as quick as possible,' said Les, 'The quicker we get this over with, the quicker we can get things back on an even keel but what's the rush?'

'It's important, we have to make all the arrangements as quick as possible,' said Doug.

'What for? To bury the evidence?' asked Shameless.

Doug shook his head, 'According to the undertakers, Mr Shufflebottom was well known as a Seven Day Adventist - a senior member of their community, that's why he could never come to many games.'

'I did know anything about that,' said Les.

'Well, it's important,' said Doug, 'We need to honour his beliefs. He needs to be buried within a week of passing.'

'I suppose that's what he'd want,' said Les.

'Oh, I don't know,' said Kenneth, 'I don't agree with Seven Day Adventists at all.'

'What are you talking about?' asked Les, 'What do you know about anything like that?'

Kenneth bristled, 'I know what people do want, I can tell you, they want more windows in their Advent calendars, not less. Mark my words, in my book it's just another example of shrinkflation - seven days will never catch on. They'll never get anywhere with an idea like that.'

Les shook his head in disbelief, 'The more *we all get involved*, the easier it'll be to come to terms with this terrible tragedy.'

'What about songs?' asked Shameless, 'What should we have at the funeral? The right music will cheer everybody up.'

'We need something that he would have wanted,' suggested Doug.

'Well, I know he was certainly a massive David Bowie fan,' said Les, 'He went over to Vegas to see him play that first live gig over there.'

'How about Breaking Glass?' asked Shameless. Daisy let out a piercing wailing shriek as Brenda tried to comfort her. Doug looked dumbstruck. He could feel his strength ebbing away. *This was clearly a challenging time.*

9. Helping Out At The Menagerie

EARLY THE NEXT MORNING Shameless reported next-door, round at the zoo to find out firsthand what needed to be done to help Laura out until all the legal business with her Mum and the death of Mr Shufflebottom had been sorted out.

'Thanks for this Shameless,' said Laura, 'For helping out like this. We really do appreciate it.'

'It's no problem love,' said Shameless, 'It'll be a change of scene.'

'Have you got any experience with animals?' asked Laura.

'Well, I've had to deal with that lot next-door for long enough.'

'You know where all the food is don't you? That's the main thing. There isn't much else to do really. Just make sure they all get the right food and you shouldn't have too many problems.'

'It's exactly the same next door,' grinned Shameless.

'We've got automatic water feeds in every cage. If ever I'm not here, just check they're all working before you lock up for the night. You shouldn't need to mess about with clean bedding but there's plenty of straw in the barn if you need any.'

'All the animals look in pretty good shape,' said Shameless.

'There aren't too many problems. There's an octopus in the aquarium with a sore tentacle. The only other issue we've got at the moment is the sperm whale.' Laura pointed to a nearby pool. Shameless was surprised to see the creature's giant head poking out over the concrete edge of the pool and resting on the side. The animal looked listless and its eyes were glazed. Shameless walked over to the animal and started gently rubbing the whale's nose.

'One thing I've always wondered,' said Shameless, 'Why is it that they're called sperm whales?'

'I wouldn't...' stuttered Laura as she struggled to find the appropriate words.

Suddenly there was a massive ejaculation from the water. Shameless groaned in horror as he was covered head-to-toe in several gallons of sperm.

10. The Arrest

A FEW DAYS LATER, two young looking police officers turned up at the ground. They spoke to Brenda briefly, then took her away in handcuffs. Kenneth and Doug looked on as she was bundled into the back of a police car.

'This doesn't look good,' said Kenneth.

'It's certainly going to be an ordeal for her,' said Doug. 'I know her family have had a lot of run-ins with the law, but I doubt she's ever been in trouble before.'

Kenneth felt scorn turning into contempt in the core of his soul, 'It's a total travesty this is,' he shouted, 'It's total police brutality! That's what it is. Stop police brutality!'

'Don't take it too hard son,' said Doug, 'They're bound to go easy on her.'

'Go easy on her? I hope they throw away the key.'

'Don't you like her?'

'We might get a decent cook for once, once they've locked her up. I for one have had enough of burnt offerings I can tell you. Pies full of broken glass? Liquorice tart? It's a wonder she hasn't killed us all by now.'

'I know all that business in the last game was very embarrassing for you.'

'Embarrassing? I'll never live it down. Where I do my business is my business. And I don't want it broadcasting on live television, thank you very much. I suppose you do know it's gone viral?'

'Try to put it all behind you.'

'Behind me?'

Doug immediately regretted his unfortunate choice of words.

'Every army marches on its stomach, you know?' said Kenneth, 'If we got fed properly, we'd probably be looking at promotion by now.'

The two men watched as the police car was driven through the carpark gates. Brenda stared out of the back window, her face was white and her eyes were dimmed with fear at the thought of what might lay ahead. Her only consolation was that at her age, life imprisonment wasn't as long as it might have been to her younger self. She'd been cooking all these years and as far as she knew, this was her very first fatality. Perhaps it was just bad luck, or perhaps it'd really been down to good luck that she'd gone this long without actually killing anyone.

11. Final Preparations

DOUG AND KENNETH WALKED STRAIGHT INTO THE OFFICE without knocking. Doug was keen to report back to Les, to let him know all about Brenda being arrested. Les was slouched over his desk. He appeared to be in some sort of trance, his gaze was fixed firmly on a serious looking invoice. He spontaneously clasped his harrowed face with both hands. He didn't seem to notice that anyone had walked through the door.

Doug paused briefly, realising that Les was highly stressed. He didn't want to add to the stress, but after weighing things up for a few seconds, he realised he really had no choice.

'The police have been, they've taken Brenda away.'

'They're charging her with manslaughter,' said Les nonchalantly as he glanced up at Doug and Kenneth.

Kenneth shuddered in revulsion, 'What do you think will happen to her?'

'Well, there's got to be mitigating circumstances,' said Doug, 'It wasn't deliberate, was it?'

'I've got a proper brief for her,' said Les, 'Although God knows how we'll afford him, the prices they charge. I just hope he turns out to be as brief as possible.'

Doug opened his mobile phone and placed a call, 'We need to do everything we can to support her.'

Les shook his head and threw the piece of paper he was holding across the desk, 'At least they've released the body. We'll soon get this funeral out of the way. Kenneth, do you think you and some of the lads would help carry the coffin?'

Kenneth nodded, 'It'll be an honour. The least I can do.'

After a brief conversation, Doug closed his phone with a grimace.

Les was good at identifying when something wasn't going well, after all, he'd had years of practice, 'Something wrong?'

Doug felt yet another wave of failure, 'That was the Gazette. I wanted to put something in the Family Notices, in case anyone local wants to know about the arrangements. But they reckon we've missed the *deadline*.'

'Typical,' said Kenneth.

'Well, if you put something together,' said Les, 'I'll take it round to their office. The proprietor was a close friend and one of Mr Shufflebottom's business associates. I'm sure he'll be able to help us out when I explain things to him.'

Doug picked up a pencil and opened a notepad. He chewed at the pencil as he tried to decide what to write, 'Have you noticed how people always say the dear departed passed away peacefully and he'll be sadly missed by one and all?'

'What else can they say?' asked Kenneth.

'No one ever says he died howling like a banshee, and we're all glad to see the back of the miserable bastard,' said Doug.

'Well, he might have died howling,' said Les, 'I guess we'll never know. But I can tell you one thing for certain, we're definitely going to miss this guy.'

'We'll never get another owner like him,' said Doug, 'Putting loads of money in every month like he did, and leaving us to get on with things without so much as a by your leave.'

'All the more reason to give the man a fitting sendoff,' said Kenneth.

12. A Final Journey

KENNETH RODE IN THE HEARSE WITH LES AND DOUG on the way to the funeral service. They were seated immediately behind the driver in the enormous, black limousine. This was a man of a very advanced age. He was very small, very thin and he looked extremely frail. His diminutive appearance seemed further exaggerated by the colossal size of the vehicle he was driving.

Kenneth was fascinated by the chauffeur's rather bizarre uniform. He was wearing an extra tall top-hat which wouldn't have been possible had he been even an inch taller. It was clearly too big for him, coming as it did at least half way down over his ears. It wasn't very wide but it got wider towards the top and it was festooned with black tassels. The entire effect seemed to be a reminder of a previous age. It looked like something that might have been worn by a mid-west newspaper tycoon or a Victorian railroad baron in eighteenth century America. Perhaps that was the point? Kenneth wondered if maybe it was a way of providing comfort to the bereaved, to signal that the deceased had reached the end of their time, that in some way they belonged to another age that had somehow already passed by.

The outfit he was wearing certainly exaggerated the driver's somewhat macabre appearance, further enhanced by a rather faded black eyepatch which was strapped partially covering his left eye. A bushy grey-white (mostly white) moustache, and deathly sallow, pale yellow, deep wrinkled skin added further to his ghoulish, rather Gothic, almost pantomime appearance and further betrayed the extremity of his age. He looked for all the world like a bit part actor out of a 1930's low budget, black-and-white, b-movie horror film. But the funeral company certainly appeared to have full confidence in him. There was no one else from the undertakers to assist him in any way.

The atmosphere inside the vehicle was bleak to say the least. All three mourners were in a very sombre mood, fully aware of the coffin that was on display at the rear of the vehicle immediately behind them.

'I hate funerals,' said Doug, 'They're always so final.'

'There's certainly never any doubt about the outcome,' said Les. 'I don't feel so good myself.'

'What's wrong with you?' asked Doug.

'It's always the same when I go to a funeral. I've got a real bad throat. How are you feeling?'

'I think I've got it as well,' said Doug, 'I feel terrible.'

Les turned to Kenneth, 'Kenneth do you think you'd be able to say a few words at the service? Give an address like.'

'I suppose I could read out your speech,' said Kenneth.

'I haven't got anything prepared as such,' croaked Les, 'I was just going to wing it.'

'Oh, I don't know,' said Kenneth, 'What would I say?'

'You've been at the club long enough,' said Doug, 'As the most senior player you're the obvious choice. He's been a good owner. Just say what comes into your head.'

'If you're sure?' said Kenneth, 'I never saw much of him.'

Les tried unsuccessfully to clear his throat, 'You knew the man as much as any of us.'

'I suppose.'

'He's always been a bit of a recluse. Nobody saw much of him. Just make some shit up. Nobody will know any different.'

The hearse cruised slowly along a winding country lane, pitching from side to side as it rolled around the bends. Kenneth looked out of the window, contemplating what he might say in his eulogy. As they progressed slowly down the lane, some enormous weeping willow trees came into view. They stood majestically on both sides of the carriageway. Their long tendrils brushed the vehicle as they cruised under them. All three mourners were struck by this poignant beauty. Les even commented on how appropriate they seemed. Kenneth stared intently, hoping beyond hope that he might find some inspiration from somewhere for his soliloquy.

After a couple of miles, the stand of willow trees ended and gave way to some fish ponds where there was a sign adverting "Coarse Fishing". As they passed by, they caught sight of a man who looked like he was suffering some kind of breakdown. His clothes were torn and his hair was wild. He was shouting and swearing and firing a twelve-bore shotgun repeatedly into a pond. Kenneth wondered if things like this went on in other parts of the country as well.

A few miles further along they passed an infant school. Outside the school there was a sign that read, "Slow Children".

'Me and Shameless went to that school,' said Kenneth.

'You do surprise me,' replied Doug.

'A lad in our class went on to become a famous writer,' said Kenneth, 'He wrote comedies for the BBC and all sorts.'

'Really? What's his name?' asked Les.

'Oh, I can't remember what they call him,' said Kenneth, 'But he is very well known. He wrote a comedy series for kids. Everybody knows about him.'

'I bet he's earned a few bob,' said Les.

'I'd think so,' said Kenneth, 'I heard he'd suffered some kind of breakdown in the end. Apparently, he had something called writers' block. It's funny, isn't it? When you think about it, all them writers who've complained about writers' block, and not a single one of them has ever written anything about it. Not a single word.'

Kenneth still hadn't thought of anything to say by the time they'd reached the church.

13. Unlucky For Some

THE FUNERAL PARTY GATHERED AROUND THE HEARSE exchanging pleasantries as they waited outside the church for an earlier funeral service to come to an end.

'It'll not be long,' reassured the driver of the hearse, 'I know they've got a slightly unusual interment, but they'll be out soon.'

Eventually, a large group of people began to emerge from the church. Everybody looked to see what was happening but they were all rather puzzled by the proceedings they were witnessing. At first there didn't appear to be a coffin. Kenneth was the first to spot it, 'Bloody hell, look at that!'

Quite a few people gasped in amazement. There was a coffin after all, in amongst the throng. But it had a most unusual shape. It was little more than two inches high and it was about four feet wide. At least a dozen people were involved in carrying the casket and it was obvious they were all struggling under the weight.

'What happened to him?' asked Les.

'He's the bloke who was run over by that steamroller,' replied the driver, 'We've had to bring in quite a few casual staff to deal with him. I'd better pop over and see if they need anyone else to lend a hand.' With that the driver scurried off to join his colleagues as they grappled with the unusual sarcophagus they had suspended above their heads.

Kenneth recognised one of the pall bearers who looked like he was struggling with an oversized flatpack wardrobe, 'He was big boned wasn't he love?'

'He certainly was. I could hardly walk after our first date.'

Les blushed heavily and took his handkerchief out of his pocket to wipe more perspiration from his furrowed brow.

By now there were quite a few people assembled around the hearse, ready to attend Mr Shufflebottom's funeral. Some of them looked very well healed. Les wondered if any of them might be interested in making any kind of investment in the club. If so, it would be very important to avoid any further embarrassment. Things were difficult enough as it was. They needed to be ready to grasp any chance of survival no matter how slim the odds were against their ongoing viability. He just hoped he hadn't made a big mistake by asking Kenneth to say a few words, but it was too late to change things now. Besides he didn't have anyone else lined up to do the job.

As the previous congregation gradually filtered out of the church, a chimneysweep suddenly emerged dressed in the traditional bowler hat. It was clear to everyone that this was all part of the sendoff. The sweep had soot smeared around his face but the rest of his clothes were spotlessly clean and he was carrying his neat brushes up against his shoulder, in a ceremonial fashion, like a guardsman carrying a rifle. Most people had seen this sort of thing at weddings but it was the first time anybody had seen anything like this at a funeral.

'He must have been in the trade,' said Les to no one in particular.

The chimneysweep followed the large flat coffin as it was manhandled out of the church. Kenneth didn't recognise the chap but thought this was too good an opportunity to miss.

'Aye! I need a word with you!' shouted Kenneth, 'I wonder if you'd be interested in doing my chimney? It's badly in need of a clean out I can tell you.'

'Oh, I don't do chimneys,' said the sweep, 'These are the only brushes I've got.'

The Chimney Sweep pointed at the short brushes he was carrying, 'This is all makeup.'

Les tried to shut Kenneth up but Kenneth was unstoppable, 'So you're just an act like?'

'My grandfather was a real sweep. I haven't cleaned a chimney in my life. No call for it these days. Nobody burns coal anymore. I just do funerals and weddings. Everybody's got central heating these days.'

'Do you get many of these gigs?'

'We've been dead busy. You wouldn't chuckle. I blame Mary Poppins myself. It's that generation you see, they're all starting to pop off.'

'Well, I think it's ridiculous,' said Doug, 'Grown men dressing up like that. Who'd ever do anything as daft as that?'

Les was quick to pick up the signs of danger. He didn't like the way this was going. The were a lot more of them than there were in his "team", and some of them looked like they could handle themselves. The last thing he needed was any kind of trouble; not when he was on the lookout for a stakeholder.

Suddenly there was a commotion from the lychgate, at the entrance to the church yard. It was Shameless! He came running up the driveway dressed in his mascot suit. Several cats shot out of the yard, running for their lives as they saw what they thought was an overgrown dog bounding towards the church.

Les gasped in horror, 'What the hell do you think you're wearing?'

'You told me to wear my best suit,' countered Shameless, 'Well this is the best suit I've got.'

Les turned to Doug, 'You need to get him sorted pronto.'

Doug grabbed Shameless by the shoulders, 'You can't go into a funeral service dressed like that you berk. The press are here, we'll end up a complete laughing stock.'

'I don't suppose you've got anything on underneath that?' asked Kenneth. His large floppy ears fluttered in the breeze as Shameless shook his head.

'Where can we get some proper clothes for him?' asked Les.

'We're going to have to think outside the box,' said Doug.

'You mean the coffin?' asked Shameless.

'He doesn't mean this box,' said Les.

Shameless looked confused. 'Which box then?'

Kenneth threw his head back as a solution unexpectedly occurred to him, 'There is a perfectly good suit in that box though.'

Les grimaced, 'You don't mean?'

'No one will be any the wiser,' said Kenneth. 'Besides, have you got a better idea?'

'Pity we haven't got a screwdriver,' said Doug.

'There's a toolbox in the back of the hearse,' said Kenneth, 'Quick! before the driver comes back.'

Les nodded his approval and with that Kenneth and Doug set about unscrewing the coffin's lid. They were surprised just how easy it was to open up.

'There isn't much to keep them in, is there?' remarked Kenneth.

As expected, Mr Shufflebottom was immaculately well dressed. Together Doug and Les carefully removed the suit from the corpse. Meanwhile Kenneth helped Shameless out of his dog costume and within a matter of minutes the makeover had been completed. For all the world this scruffy caretaker-cum-groundsman gave the appearance of being a long-standing member of the jet set, as he stood there in Mr Shufflebottom's best suit; a suit that had been skilfully crafted from the very finest Cashmere cloth. The transformation was amazing. Just a few minutes earlier, Shameless had looked like an extra in a cut-price backstreet amateur theatre production - he now looked like the Manager Director of a top city brokers. Kenneth admired this amazing sartorial elegance as Les and Doug hastily screwed the coffin lid back into place and stuffed the dog suit under the back seat in the hearse.

14. A Service To Remember

LES, DOUG AND SHAMELESS were led into the church by the driver. They took up seats that had been specially reserved for them at the front of the alter, whilst Kenneth waited by the hearse, ready to help the other pallbearers to carry the coffin in for the service. He glanced at his watch and looked down the lane, hoping to see the rest of the team, but he couldn't see anyone else coming. He tried as hard as he could to supress his nerves but he couldn't help it, he felt himself starting to feel anxious, 'I hope someone comes soon.'

A few minutes later the driver returned back to where Kenneth was waiting. 'I'm sorry, we can't wait any longer, there's another service straight after this one.'

'It looks like it's just the two of us then?' said Kenneth weakly.

'Oh no, I'm sorry. I can't carry anything, not with my back and everything. Besides, I'm a fully paid-up member of Unite. They'd come down on me like a ton of bricks if I stepped out of line. I'm a driver Gov, strictly transport, lifting and shifting is definitely not part of my skillset. I'm sorry, you're on your own with this one.'

'Then can you go and ask some of the others to help me please?'

'I'd get a shift on if I were you. This pastor is a stickler for punctuality. He won't stand for any nonsense. If he sees any shilly-shallying he'll blow you out, no mistake about that. On your head be it, that's all I'm saying.'

Kenneth knew there was only one thing for it, 'Well can you get the doors for me?'

'Strictly speaking I shouldn't. I don't normally do anything like that, but go on, seeing as it's you I'm prepared to turn a blind eye. Just this once mind.'

Kenneth opened the back of the hearse and groaned in pain as he slid the coffin out of the rear door. He managed to pull the casket into his arms, then staggered gasping into the church, carrying the heavy wooden box all on his own. The driver did hold the church doors open for him as promised, and shouted at mourners to clear the way as Kenneth staggered up the aisle. His was a monumental effort. It caused him to sweat profusely, only a professional sportsman could have attempted anything like this, but after a great deal of grunting and groaning, he eventually made his way up towards the alter with the casket clutched awkwardly in his arms. Everybody was amazed by this incredible feat of strength but nobody came to help him. Eventually he reached the plinth in front of the alter, where he finally received some assistance from the clergy and the organist who helped to manoeuvre the coffin into place.

'Blinking heck. I can't belief I had to do that on my own,' moaned Kenneth. 'He certainly didn't die of hunger; I can tell you that.'

Les sighed in disbelief as he belatedly caught sight of Kenneth completing his mission, 'Where the hell are the rest of them?'

Doug shrugged. The celebrant was clearly in a hurry, he whispered something to Kenneth who then climbed up onto to the alter ready to deliver his eulogy to the assembled multitude. He was still gasping for breath and paused briefly whilst he gathered his thoughts.

At this point Brenda who was seated in the second row noticed Shameless in his newly acquired smart suit.

'You're a dark horse, aren't you?' Brenda hissed at Shameless.

'Am I?' asked Shameless, somewhat perplexed by the comment.

'I always wondered how you managed to hold your job down.'

Shameless looked confused. 'What are you talking about?'

'You. You're such a lazy bugger. I always wondered how you never got the sack.'

Les picked up on the conversation. 'It's the tie you fool,' he explained to Shameless.

Brenda fluttered her eyelashes as she smiled admiringly at the motif tie which Shameless had fastened tight around his neck.

'I never knew you were a tadpole as well,' said Brenda. 'That might well come in handy in the days ahead, with the way things are.'

Up on the alter Kenneth cleared his throat and belatedly won the attention of the congregation.

After a brief pause, he began his address, 'As you all know, Mr Shufflebottom was a very generous man. He had money, but he was a good man, a very good man in fact. He always used his money in a very good way, for very good things and that made him a very good man.'

Les leaned over and whispered to Doug, 'See. I knew he'd be alright. He's not making a bad job of it, is he?'

Doug bowed grudgingly before shrugging slightly and rather sheepishly nodding his agreement.

'And what's more,' shouted Kenneth, 'He did a lot for the community. Not only did he support us, *your one-and-only truly local football team*, he also did lots of other things for the community. Not everybody knows this, but it was Mr Shufflebottom himself who arranged the clap for the NHS round these parts, which, given the number of times he'd received medication for that particular condition, always seemed particularly appropriate.'

On hearing these words, there was a loud gasp from the congregation as they expressed shock and outrage in response to Kenneth's breathtaking proclamation.

Les almost choked. He hissed at Doug in blind panic, 'For God's sake, get him off.'

Doug rushed up to the alter and pulled the microphone away from Kenneth, then with the help of the minister and several of the larger choir boys, he managed to bundle Kenneth off the alter and into the pews next to Les.

It was left to the celebrant to recover the situation. Addressing the congregation he said, 'Thank you very much Kenneth for that touching, er, I mean heartfelt tribute on this very sad occasion, to our dear friend and colleague who will of course be very greatly missed by one and all.'

But Kenneth felt affronted and continued to scuffle with Doug in the pews.

'Kenneth! Kenneth! Calm yourself down Kenneth,' snarled Les, 'Show a bit of respect.'

Kenneth pushed Doug away and calmed himself. He blushed heavily, as he realised just how dishevelled he was and the fact that he'd caused such a scene in front of so many people. He hurriedly re-arranged his clothing and tried to recover something of his dignity and self-respect.

Les was most indignant. He was equally angry with both Kenneth and Doug for showing the club up with such a terrible display like that. 'Bloody hell, we've got Brenda's committal hearing at the end of the week. We don't want to make things any worse than they already are, do we? Surely you can understand that?'

'What?' said Kenneth, 'You mean worse than murder?'

Les turned around to make sure no one else was listening, 'Now listen you two. I think it's only fair to warn you, the judge has told us to prepare ourselves to expect the worst. It's important! Get a grip. We really need to show some discipline, to prove to the general public that we're a respectable slide who have made an unintentional mistake; not some kind of rabble who haven't a clue how to behave. Think on. We don't want to make the worst any worse, do we?'

'What do you mean?' said Kenneth, 'Do you think they might let her off?'

Les shook his head in contempt. 'The best thing you can do is pray we don't all get sent down. I wouldn't like to say how this is all going to turn out. Mr S had some very powerful friends in some very high places. The police are still investigating. We'll be lucky if any of us get off completely scot-free.'

The service continued with the reading of psalm 23 verse 4 and a rendition of 'Heart of Glass' by the local choir.

The rest of the service was concluded without drama, and there was relief all round when the interment was brought to a successful conclusion. Afterwards thoughts quickly turned to the court ordeal that lay ahead. Les wanted to make sure that any damage to the reputation of the club should be avoided as much as possible. He knew this would be important if they were to have any hope of finding any kind of new benefactor.

Les also wanted to do everything possible to try to make sure all the mitigating factors were fully taken into account so that Brenda would receive the lightest possible sentence. He knew they could have done with Mr Shufflebottom's presence in these circumstances, but although that was no longer possible, he hoped that the authorities would realise that their owner's sad demise was nothing more sinister than a tragic accident, and not something that involved any kind of bad feeling or malice, or any kind of malicious intent. After all, everyone at the club had benefited from Mr Shufflebottom's stewardship and couldn't possibly have any reason to wish him harm. It was like a cup match; time would tell *but there would only ever be one chance to get this right.*

15. The Day Of Reckoning.

BRENDA STOOD NERVOUSLY in the dock of the court, as she waited for the proceedings to commence. Les, Doug and Kenneth walked in accompanied by Brenda's barrister. He was a tall, heavily set young man with an easy manner and a superior smile, who exuded an air of confidence. The barrister clutched a small bundle of papers which he pressed tightly to the left side of his breast. Apparently, he'd known Mr Shufflebottom very well and was well aware of the precarious financial status of the club.

Daisy, Laura and Tallulah shuffled in through the door. Daisy was dressed in her Sunday best but the two sisters looked rather bedraggled. They clearly hadn't slept well for days. Halfway up the courtroom the three of them came to an abrupt halt. They weren't certain where they should sit. A court usher noticed their confusion and came to their assistance. He escorted them to seats right at the front, as close to the dock as it was possible to be.

Brenda's face lifted when she finally caught sight of Daisy and her daughters. She waved her finger, not really knowing if such a thing were allowed in a courtroom, and she tried her best to raise a smile. But the overriding sense of dread that she was experiencing meant she was unable to do little more than pout. She realised this shortcoming and after a few failed attempts, she gave up trying to smile. This made her feel emotional, but after gathering herself, she decided instead that it was best to nod her head in the direction of her daughters in recognition of their support. Whatever happened, at least she felt some comfort from the fact her own flesh and blood would be able to walk free and tell the tale of this terrible tragedy.

Everybody stood as the lady judge entered from the top end of the courtroom and took her place on the imposing, leather-bound throne at the front. 'Order!' shouted the chief usher. The courtroom fell silent and once the judge was seated, everybody sat down except Brenda who desperately clutched the railings around the dock to stop herself from falling over.

The judge glanced around and caught sight of Kenneth and Doug, who were both sporting black eyes and bruising across their faces; souvenirs from their fracas at the funeral a few days earlier. She shook her head in disgust. This reaction from the judge caused Laura in particular, a great deal of concern. She felt a deep sense of foreboding which struck her like a thunderbolt. She was very concerned, *what must this judge be thinking?*

Les noticed Laura's discomfort. He leaned over to her and in hushed tones he comforted her, 'It'll be alright love. There's nothing to worry about.'

'I've left Shameless in charge of the wildlife park. I hope he'll be alright.'

'Don't worry about him,' said Doug, 'He'll be having a whale of a time.'

'Just try to keep calm,' said Les, 'We can always appeal if we need to.'

Suddenly Kenneth stood up, 'Don't worry Brenda love. We're all behind you!' he shouted. A ripple of laughter ran through the court as people spotted his t-shirt which sported the slogan, "Choose Life".

Les and Doug were mortified. The judge was livid. She banged her gavel, 'Shut down and sit up. Any more outbursts like that and I'll have you sent down.'

Everybody had noticed her slip, but everybody was too afraid to smirk. This judge clearly meant business and she wasn't one to be trifled with.

It was all a bit too much for Brenda who started snivelling loudly, 'I'm very, very sorry. I really am very sorry.'

'How would you like to plead?' asked the judge.

'To be honest, I'd like to plead innocent. And I would if I hadn't done it, really, I would.'

'Thank you,' said the judge, 'I'll record that response as guilty. Well, I've taken into account all the circumstances. Clearly this was an appalling lapse of judgement. But I'm satisfied from the written submissions that there genuinely was no malicious intent, and I can see no evidence to the contrary. Mr Brown, can I call on the prosecution to confirm your position on this matter please?'

A barrister leapt to his feet, 'I can confirm that the documents you have before you accurately reflect our conclusion in this case Your Honour, and that our view remains substantively and irrevocably unchanged.' With that the barrister resumed his seat.

'Very well, thank you Mr Brown. In view of this confirmation, I can confirm that the Crown Prosecution Service has reviewed this case and accept your admission of monumental negligence, gross incompetence and total, manifest stupidity. In any case, I can think of no greater punishment for you to serve other than you should continue to endure the appalling conditions in that terrible, total abysmal kitchen. I therefore sentence you to seventy-two hours community service. And I hope this sentence might provide some relief for you to enjoy at least some, albeit brief respite, from the truly dreadful employment you somehow manage to endure each and every day in that frightful hellhole of a kitchen.'

A wave of confusion and disbelief rippled throughout the court as people muttered to each other and tried to process everything that had just been announced by the judge.

Kenneth was most disconcerted. 'Charming, I'm sure!' he said in a voice that echoed across the chamber.

Brenda tried but failed to hold back the tears, 'Oh thank you your Ladyship, you're very kind,' she snivelled into her now very damp hanky.

All eyes were on Brenda. Everybody felt relieved but they also felt sorry for her. It was left to Doug to lift the mood. 'Come on Brenda love, cheer up, you're a free woman!' he roared.

The clerk of the court glanced at the judge, wondering if it was worth trying to call everyone to order but the judge simply shook her head. 'You're free to go,' she announced.

Brenda walked out of the court being comforted by Les who had his arm round her shoulder. Likewise, Kenneth tried to comfort Daisy. Laura and Talulah followed behind with Doug and Kenneth and the rest of the entourage.

'It's a miracle Les,' said Brenda, 'It's Mr Shufflebottom who's done this, I'm sure of it.'

'Happen love. I wouldn't be surprised. He always had friends in high places.'

'I think he's a saint. He always was really, when you think about it. I'd like to visit his grave if I could, to pay my respects and everything, if you think that might be possible?'

'It might give you some closure Mum,' said Laura, 'You'll be able to see him at rest. Hopefully it'll bring this entire tragic nightmare to an end.'

'I'm sure we could visit the grave,' said Les.

'No time like the present,' said Doug.

'We can go now if you like?' said Les, 'Do you think you'd be up to it?'

Brenda nodded through her snivels. 'I'd like to make sure that he's satisfied with the way things have turned out.'

Doug raised his eyes at Les. *How could any victim ever be satisfied with their murder?* Les's mouth dropped in response, but he knew he had to focus on Brenda, 'We'll go round straight away love. I'm sure he'd want us all to show our respects now we've got everything settled at long last.'

16. A Fitting Memorial

LES DROVE BRENDA AND DAISY the short distance around to the cemetery. Doug followed behind in his car with Kenneth, Laura and Tallulah on board. Brenda was clearly nervous about the visit, but she felt it was something she had to do to *try to put things right.* They pulled straight into the cemetery carpark where they parked with ease as the place was deserted.

'It looks different,' said Doug, 'When there's no one here.'

'It's over there,' said Les pointing to the newest grave with lots of wreathes positioned around it. 'It's amazing, look at that, they didn't waste any time getting that put up.'

'I thought it best to get it done as soon as possible,' said Doug, 'I wasn't quite sure if it was part of the seven-day thing, so I thought it best to play it safe.'

'Who did you use?'

'I got them builders on Freehold Street. They don't mess about and they were cheap - five hundred quid all in, including the granite, the engraving and installation. And the best thing is they did it straight away, without any delay.'

'It sounds like a bargain,' said Kenneth, 'I'm sure he'd be pleased.'

Les linked arms with Brenda and they all ambled solemnly over to the grave with as much dignity as they could muster.

'It's a beautiful memorial,' said Brenda as she moved around to the front of the grave to read the inscription.

Then suddenly, without any warning Brenda let out a tremendous gasp of horror. Doug was the first to realise what had caused such a reaction and he turned away in embarrassment. His face instantly glowed bright deep scarlet and then darkened almost to purple.

'I've never seen anything like it,' said Brenda, with a faltering voice.

'Good God,' gulped Kenneth as he too caught sight of the engraving.

Les shouted angrily at Doug, 'I've told you before about texting everything, haven't I?'

Kenneth began to read the inscription out loud, 'Mr Stephen Spencer Shufflebottom 1929 - 2023'

Les stepped back in shock, struggling to maintain his balance.

Brenda continued reading, 'Please leave the lower half blank. Les can't have much time left and we'll save a few bob if we leave room for that prat as well. GTG.'

Kenneth pointed to the bottom of the stone and read the last line, 'Sent from my Huawei phone!'

Les shook his head, 'Bloody hell Doug!'

--- THE END ---

Printed in Great Britain
by Amazon